To my family –
Thanks for creating a strong foundation
of love, kindness, and support.
- A.B.

For my family.
- T.B.

Text copyright © 2021 by Happiness Forward LLC

Written by: Arianna Brooks
Illustrated by: Torey Butner
ISBN: 978-1-7365942-1-6
Library of Congress Control Number: 2021912627
First Edition

Visit Carissa the Crane and the Construction Crew:
www.carissathecrane.com

CARISSA THE CRANE

AND THE CONSTRUCTION CREW
A Rock & Roll Construction Story

written by Arianna Brooks
illustrated by Torey Butner

 Happiness Forward LLC

A site in Chicago,
not long ago...

Is where we
begin our

ROCK
& ROLL
SHOW

Humming high above the ***whoosh whoosh*** of the train

Presenting our star...
CARISSA
THE CRANE!

The construction crew *clang clang* on the scene

Bouncing along to a singing machine

"I have an idea, let's all gather near

We should play music together right here!"

Mason starts with a

WHIRL, WHIRL

on repeat

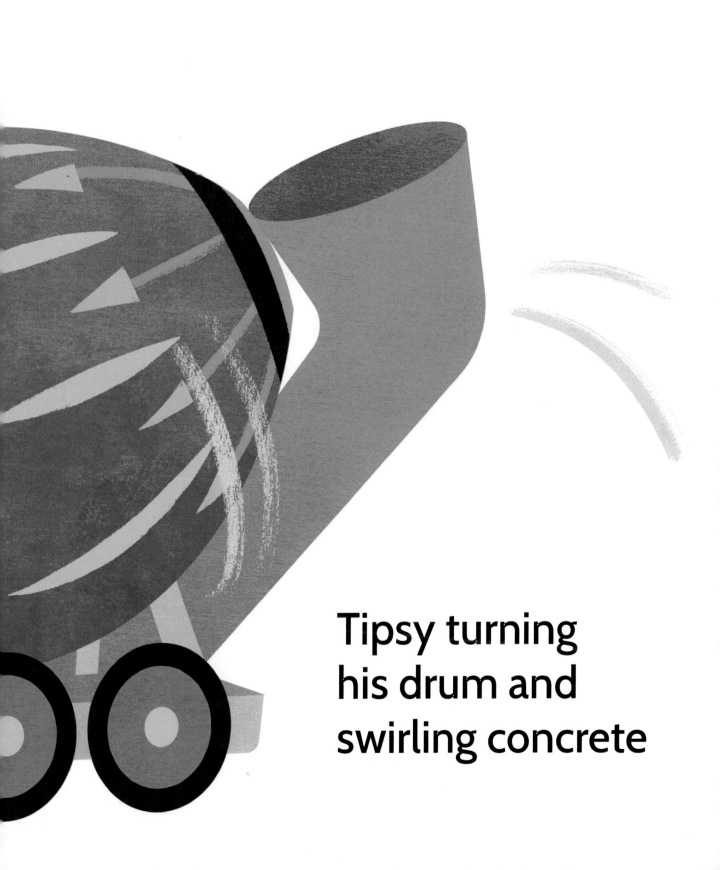

Tipsy turning
his drum and
swirling concrete

Emma lifts her bucket,
just like a guitar

then digs up the ground,

A TOTAL ROCKSTAR!

Next up is
Dylan, the

FUNKY
BEATBOX

Who fills up
his bed with
rubble and rocks

Dancing along to the rock & roll beat

Babies *clap* their hands

and *wiggle* their feet

Then Carissa adds a signature hook

People walking by drop everything to look

At the
crosswalk
the traffic
jams along

As Carissa *belts* out the final song

"Thank you," they say with a bow and a smile

Mighty building machines with tons of style.

Arianna Brooks knew that she had to step up her game when her son became fascinated by construction vehicles (without leaving her daughter behind). Stuck in Wrigleyville traffic with two toddlers and needing to fill the time, Carissa the Crane was born! Arianna lives and writes in Chicagoland with her family.

Torey Butner is an illustrator based in the Bay Area, California who has a passion for illustrating, writing and telling stories that create memorable experiences. She attended school in Illinois, a trains ride away from Chicago where she was drawn to the buildings, sounds and foods that make the city unique.

For more by the Brooks/Butner dream team, check out *My Mushy Matzah Ball*! www.mymushymatzahball.com

Made in the USA
Middletown, DE
21 November 2021

53101800R00015